W9-AGW-014

Pinkalicious®
and the Pinkamazing Little Library

To Pamela
—V.K.

The author gratefully acknowledges
the artistic and editorial contributions of
Daniel Griffo and Jacqueline Resnik.

I Can Read® and I Can Read Book® are trademarks of HarperCollins Publishers.

Pinkalicious and the Pinkamazing Little Library
Copyright © 2023 by VBK, Co.

PINKALICIOUS and all related logos are trademarks of VBK, Co. Used with permission.

Based on the HarperCollins book *Pinkalicious* written by
Victoria Kann and Elizabeth Kann, illustrated by Victoria Kann.
All rights reserved. Printed in the United States of America.
No part of this book may be used or reproduced in any manner whatsoever without
written permission except in the case of brief quotations embodied in critical articles and reviews.
For information address HarperCollins Children's Books, a division of HarperCollins Publishers,
195 Broadway, New York, NY 10007.
www.icanread.com

Library of Congress Control Number: 2022944215
ISBN 978-0-06-325732-0 (trade bdg.) — ISBN 978-0-06-325731-3 (pbk.)

23 24 25 26 27 LB 10 9 8 7 6 5 4 3 2 1

First Edition

Dear Parent:
Your child's love of reading starts here!

Every child learns to read in a different way and at his or her own speed. Some go back and forth between reading levels and read favorite books again and again. Others read through each level in order. You can help your young reader improve and become more confident by encouraging his or her own interests and abilities. From books your child reads with you to the first books he or she reads alone, there are I Can Read Books for every stage of reading:

SHARED READING
Basic language, word repetition, and whimsical illustrations, ideal for sharing with your emergent reader

BEGINNING READING
Short sentences, familiar words, and simple concepts for children eager to read on their own

READING WITH HELP
Engaging stories, longer sentences, and language play for developing readers

READING ALONE
Complex plots, challenging vocabulary, and high-interest topics for the independent reader

I Can Read Books have introduced children to the joy of reading since 1957. Featuring award-winning authors and illustrators and a fabulous cast of beloved characters, I Can Read Books set the standard for beginning readers.

A lifetime of discovery begins with the magical words "I Can Read!"

*Visit www.icanread.com for information
on enriching your child's reading experience.*

Pinkalicious®
and the Pinkamazing Little Library

by Victoria Kann

HARPER

An Imprint of HarperCollinsPublishers

"Are you reading AGAIN?"
Jade asked.

"Yes!" I said.

"Learning to read was hard,
but now it's pinkamazingly fun!"

I blew my nose loudly.

Honk honk!

"Is everything okay?" asked Kendra.

"This book is so sad!" I sobbed.

"Does anyone have more tissues?"
Jade asked.

"Pinkalicious is reading again!"

At lunch, I couldn't stop laughing

at my joke book.

" 'Why can't your nose

be twelve inches long?' "

I read out loud.

" 'Because then it would be a foot!' "

I read in bed.

I read at the table.

I even read while I walked.

"Whoops," I said.

"Sorry, tree!"

My book was too good
to stop for dinner.
"Yuck!" I said.
I had nibbled my napkin
instead of my pasta,
but I kept reading.
I was at the best part!

"Pinkalicious, can you please
put down your book
for a few minutes?" Daddy asked.
"I forget what you look like!"

"I can't put the book down!" I said.

"I have to find out what happens."

I read and read

until I finished the book.

"That was pinkamazing!" I said.

"Time for another book!"

When I got to my room,

I saw something very bad.

I had read every book

at least twice!

The next day,

I hurried to the library.

"I'm sorry," said the librarian.

"You've read every kids' book here!"

I couldn't believe it.

"I'M OUT OF BOOKS?" I said.

What was I going to do?

I didn't have a book

to make me laugh or cry

or eat my napkin!

"May I please get a new book?"

I begged Mommy.

"If you buy it yourself,"

Mommy said.

The problem was that

my piggy bank was empty.

I read our cereal boxes.

I read our catalogs.

I read all of Mommy's cupcake recipes.

They weren't the same.

"I need books! I want a story!" I said.

"You have books!" Peter said.

"Lots of books."

"I need NEW books," I explained.

"Too bad you can't trade yours

for new ones," Peter said.

"That's it!" I gasped.

"What's it?" Peter asked.

"Great idea!" I said.

"What idea?" he asked.

"Thanks, Peter!" I said.

"You're . . . welcome?" he said.

I spent the rest of the day

working on my project.

Finally I was all set.

"Presenting the booktastic

Pinkamazing Little Library!"

22

"People can take my books
and leave theirs," I explained.

"It was my idea," Peter said proudly.

"I think."

I made fliers to hand out.

"Calling all readers!" I said.

"Come trade your books

at my Pinkamazing Little Library!"

"I'm a reader!" Jade said.

"Me too!" Rose said.

That night,

I was too excited to sleep.

I couldn't wait to see

the new books in my library!

I tiptoed outside in the dark.

All my books were gone!

There were new books in their place.

I couldn't wait to start reading!

Pinkamazing Little Library

I was so excited that I didn't hear
Peter until he was right next to me.
"May I have a book too?" he asked.
"We want books too!" Mommy
and Daddy said.

The next morning,

we all read through breakfast.

Peter giggled at his picture book.

Daddy chuckled at his joke book.

Mommy gasped at her mystery.

I turned the last page of my book.

"Best book ever!" I said.

No one responded.

"Best book of the year!"

I added loudly.

Silence.

I looked around at my family.

They all had their noses in their books!

"Could you all put down your books

for a few minutes?" I said.

"I forget what you look like!"

"Sorry," Daddy said with a laugh.

"Oops," Mommy said.

"This book is a real page-turner!"

"I understand," I said.

"You all PINKALOVE reading
as much as I do!"